GRAYSLAKE AREA PUBLIC LIBRARY

3 6109 00314 3044

W9-AVR-121

Grayslake Area Public Library District
Grayslake, Illinois

1. A fine will be charged on each book which is not returned when it is due.

2. All injuries to books beyond reasonable wear and all losses shall be made good to the satisfaction of the Librarian.

3. Each borrower is held responsible for all books drawn on his card and for all fines accruing on the same.

NO L. GER OWNED BY
GRAYSL PUBLIC LIBRARY

DEMCO

This book belongs to:

_____

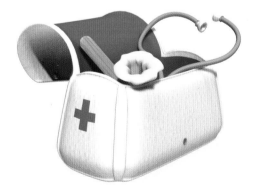

Copyright © 2007 by Callaway & Kirk Company LLC. All rights reserved.
Published by Callaway & Kirk Company, a division of Callaway Arts & Entertainment.
Miss Spider, Sunny Patch Friends, and all related characters are trademarks and/or registered
trademarks of Callaway & Kirk Company LLC, a division of Callaway Arts & Entertainment.
Callaway & Kirk Company LLC, Callaway Arts & Entertainment, and their respective logotypes
are trademarks and/or registered trademarks. All rights reserved.

Digital art by Callaway Animation Studios under the direction of David Kirk in collaboration with Nelvana Limited.

This book is based on the TV episode "The Bug Flu," written by Robin Stein, from the animated TV series
Miss Spider's Sunny Patch Friends on Nick Jr., a Nelvana Limited/Absolute Pictures Limited co-production
in association with Callaway Arts & Entertainment, based on the Miss Spider books by David Kirk.

Nicholas Callaway, President and Publisher
Cathy Ferrara, Managing Editor and Production Director
Toshiya Masuda, Art Director • Nelson Gómez, Director of Digital Technology
Joya Rajadhyaksha, Editor • Amy Cloud, Editor
Bill Burg, Digital Artist • Christina Pagano, Digital Artist
Raphael Shea, Senior Designer • Krupa Jhaveri, Designer

Special thanks to the Nelvana staff, including Doug Murphy, Scott Dyer, Tracy Ewing, Pam Lehn,
Tonya Lindo, Mark Picard, Jane Sobol, Luis Lopez, Eric Pentz, and John Cvecich.

No part of this publication may be reproduced, or stored in a retrieval system, or transmitted in any form or by any
means, electronic, mechanical, photocopying, recording, or otherwise, without written permission of the publisher.

Library of Congress Cataloging-in-Publication Data available upon request.

Distributed in the United States by Penguin Young Readers Group.

Visit Callaway Arts & Entertainment at www.callaway.com.

ISBN 978-0-448-44691-2

10 9 8 7 6 5 4 3 2 1   07 08 09 10

First edition, September 2007

Printed in China

3 6109 00314 3044

ER
Kirk,
D.
6.8K

Miss Spider's

SUNNY PATCH FRIENDS

The Bug Flu

David Kirk

CALLAWAY

NEW YORK

2007

GRAYSLAKE AREA PUBLIC LIBRARY
100 Library Lane
Grayslake, IL 60030

"Work, work, work!" Spiderus was so busy grumbling about having to pick sunflower seeds that he didn't look where he was going and tripped over a leaf!

Ha! he thought. If I pretend to be hurt, I won't have to work.

"Oh, woe! I think I injured my left third leg!" he wailed.

Shimmer, Squirt, and Dragon offered to help collect seeds so Spiderus could rest.

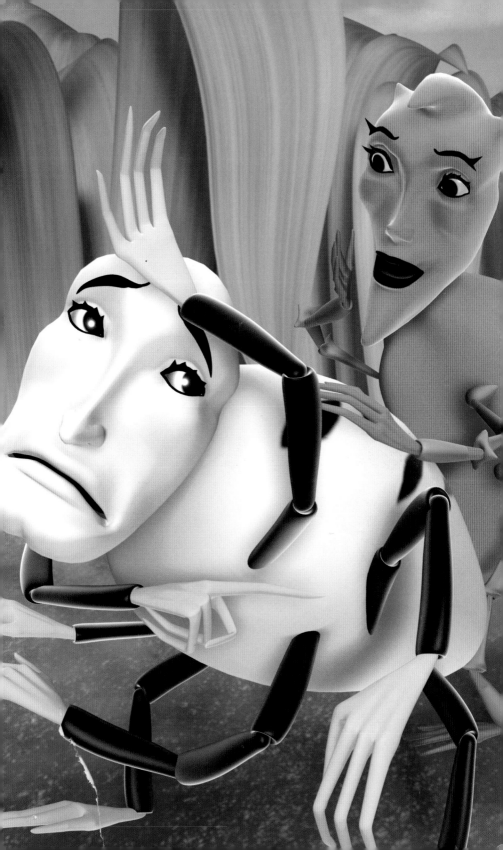

Soon, Miss Spider crawled by. "I'd like to invite your whole family to a tea party tomorrow to thank your kids for helping!" Spindella said.

"We'd love to come!" Miss Spider exclaimed.

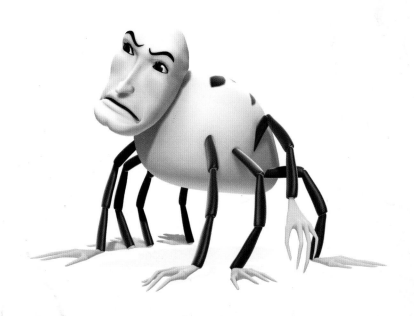

Later that afternoon, Shimmer noticed Spiderus skittering along happily by the Taddy Puddle.

"He tricked us into thinking he was hurt so we would do his work!" she cried.

"Hmm," Dragon mused, "that's a pretty cool idea."

The next day, everybuggy was getting ready to go to Spindella and Spiderus's tea party.

"It's going to be boring!" Bounce whined.

Dragon began coughing. "I don't feel so well!" he wheezed.

"You must be getting the bug flu," Miss Spider said. She decided to stay home and take care of him.

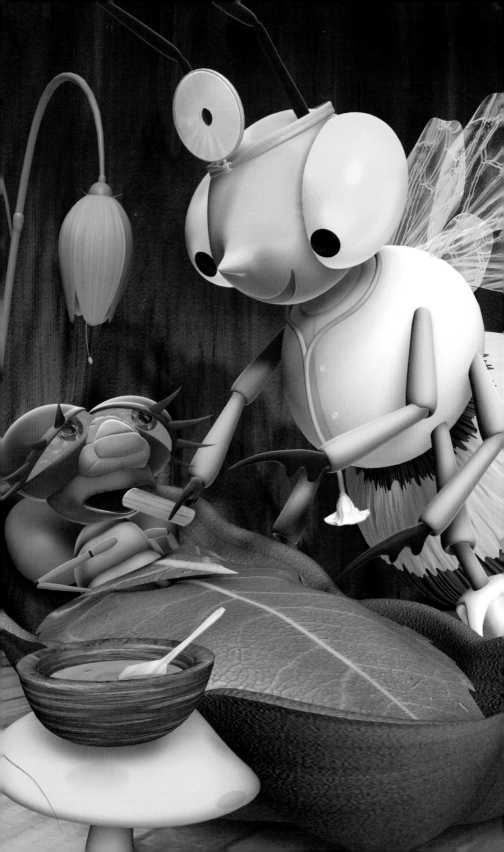

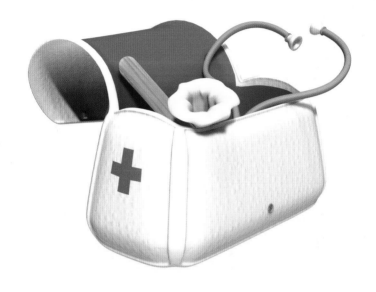

Dr. Bee Better came over. She listened to Dragon's spiracles, the holes through which dragonflies breathe. She made him open up his mouth and say, "Anthill."

"I think our little patient has a case of the Fakey Flu," Dr. Bee Better told Miss Spider.

"Hmm . . . I know just the cure for pretending to be sick!" Miss Spider said with a smile.

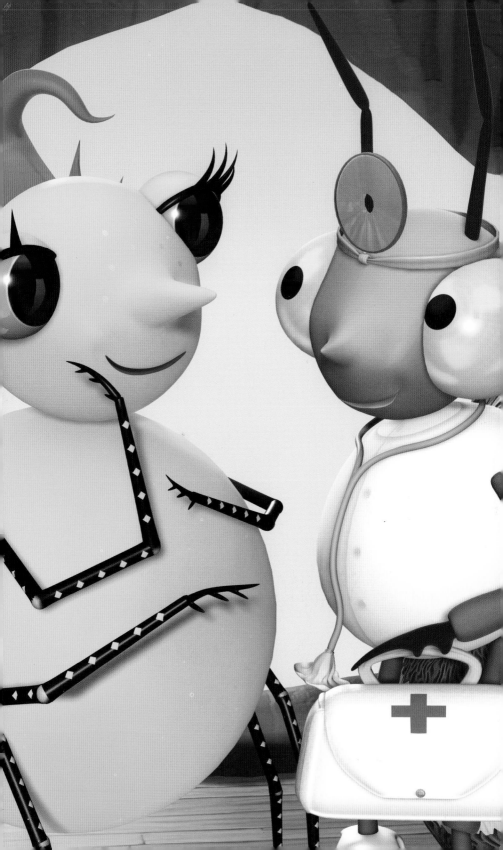

Soon the other kids came back, stuffed with sweets and still laughing. The party had been a buggy blast!

"Spindella taught us some really cool games!" Wiggle grinned.

"Let's play one now!" cried Dragon, leaping out of bed.

"Oh no, Dragon," Miss Spider said. "You're too sick to play."

"But I'm feeling better!" Dragon insisted.

"I don't think so," Holley said. "Back up to bed, li'l bug!"

So, Dragon lay alone and listened as his siblings laughed and played.

The next morning, Holley announced that the whole family would go berry picking.

"All right!" Dragon whooped. "Betcha I get the biggest berry!"

"Not so fast," said Holley. "You're still sick, and you need to rest."

After Holley and the kids had left, Dragon snuck out the window and flew to the blueberry bush. He watched everybuggy laughing and having fun.

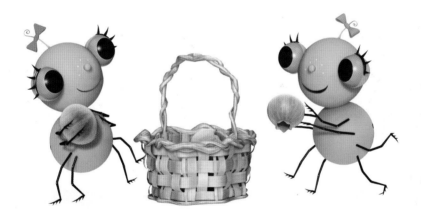

"I'm sick of being sick," he decided.

Dragon flew back into the bedroom and stopped short with a gasp. There was Miss Spider, along with Spiderus and Spindella, who had brought him some get-well cookies.

"Care to explain yourself?" his mother asked.

Dragon gulped. "I only pretended to be sick," he confessed. "I'm really sorry."

"Pretending to be sick is like telling a lie," Miss Spider said sternly. "I think you owe Spindella an apology."

"I'm sorry if I hurt your feelings, Spindella," Dragon said sheepishly.

"That's okay," Spindella said. "I'm just glad you're healthy."

"I have an idea," said Miss Spider, "a way that you can make this up to everybuggy."

The next morning, Dragon brought a big bushel of blueberries to Spindella and Spiderus.

"I picked these myself," he said proudly. "No faking!"

GRAYSLAKE AREA PUBLIC LIBRARY
100 Library Lane
Grayslake, IL 60030